The Foggy Foggy Forest

WALKER BOOKS
AND SUBSIDIARIES

LONDON · BOSTON · SYDNEY · AUCKLAND

Nick Sharratt

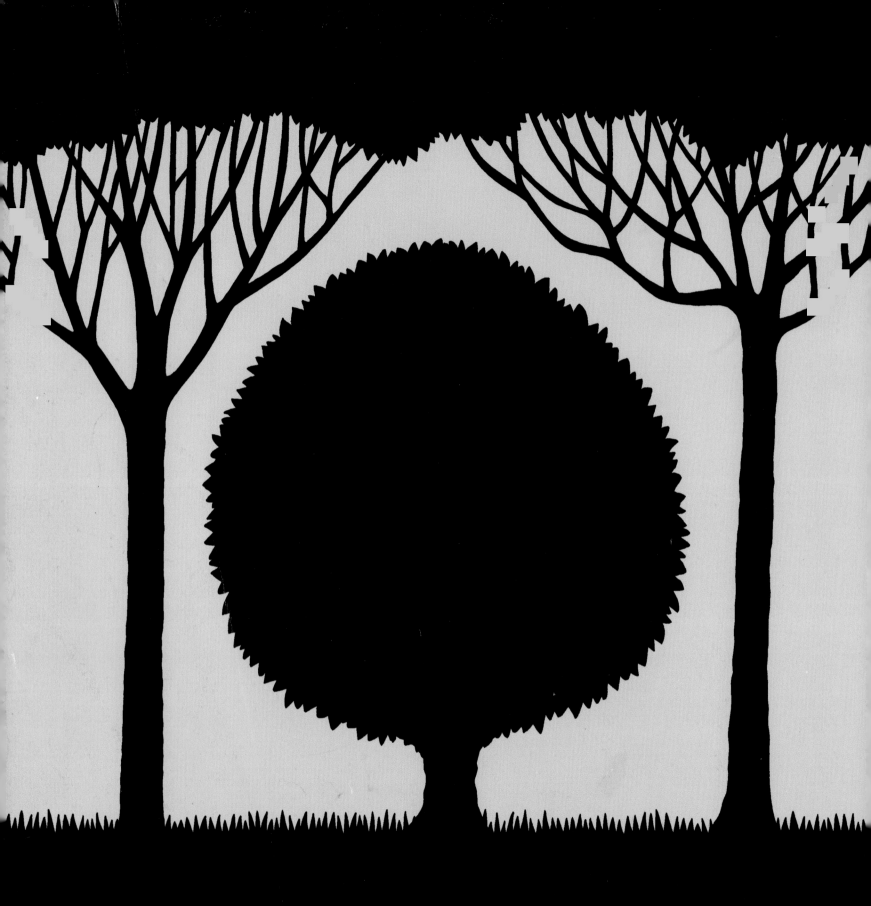

What can this be in the foggy, foggy forest?

A little elf all by himself.

What can this be in the foggy, foggy forest?

Three brown bears in picnic chairs.

What can this be in the foggy, foggy forest?

A fairy queen on a trampoline.

What can this be in the foggy, foggy forest?

A unicorn blowing a horn.

What can this be in the foggy, foggy forest?

Goldilocks with a box of chocs.

What can this be in the foggy, foggy forest?

A witch on a broom …

with an engine – vroom vroom!

What can this be in the foggy, foggy forest?

An ogre doing yoga.

What can this be in the foggy, foggy forest?

Cinderella and Snow White

in a water pistol fight.

What can this be in the foggy, foggy forest?

Little Red Riding Hood and her Gran

selling ice creams from their van.

And what can *that* be over there?

Hooray! Hooray! A travelling fair!